Jack and Jill

and friends

Miles
KeLLY

First published in 2011 by Miles Kelly Publishing Ltd
Harding's Barn, Bardfield End Green, Thaxted, Essex, CM6 3PX, UK

2 4 6 8 10 9 7 5 3 1

Editorial Director Belinda Gallagher

Art Director Jo Cowan

Editor Sarah Parkin

Cover/Junior Designer Kayleigh Allen

Production Manager Elizabeth Collins

Reprographics Stephan Davis, Ian Paulyn

ISBN 978-1-84810-411-2

Printed in China

British Library Cataloguing-in-Publication Data
A catalogue record for this book is available from the British Library

ACKNOWLEDGEMENTS

The publishers would like to thank Kirsten Wilson for
the illustration she provided for 'Ducks' Ditty'.

All other artworks are from the Miles Kelly Artwork Bank
Cover artist: Pam Smy

Made with paper from a sustainable forest

www.mileskelly.net
info@mileskelly.net
www.factsforprojects.com

Self-publish your
children's book

buddingpress.co.uk

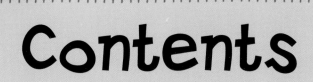

Contents

The Cat and the Fiddle

Hey diddle diddle,

The cat and the fiddle,

The cow jumped over the moon.

The little dog laughed to see such fun,

And the dish ran away with the spoon.

Three Men in a Tub

Rub-a-dub-dub,
Three men in a tub;
And who do you think they be?

The butcher, the baker,
The candlestick-maker;
They all jumped out of a rotten potato,
'Twas enough to make a man stare.

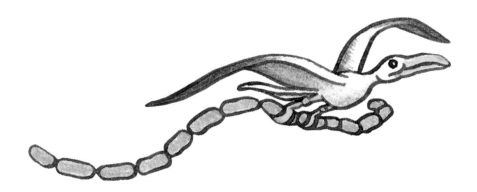

The Wheels on the Bus

The wheels on the bus
go round and round,
Round and round,
round and round.
The wheels on the bus
go round and round,
All day long.

(Roll your hands over each other)

8

The horn on the bus goes,
"Beep, beep, beep!
Beep, beep, beep!
Beep, beep, beep!"
The horn on the bus goes,
"Beep, beep, beep!"
All day long.

(Pretend to honk the horn)

The windscreen wipers go, "Swish, swish, swish! Swish, swish, swish! Swish, swish, swish!" The windscreen wipers go, "Swish, swish, swish!" All day long.

(Swish your arms like windscreen wipers)

The people on the bus bounce up and down, Up and down, up and down. The people on the bus bounce up and down, All day long.

(Bounce up and down)

The daddies on the bus go nod, nod, nod,
Nod, nod, nod, nod, nod, nod.
The daddies on the bus go
nod, nod, nod,
All day long.

(Nod your head)

The mummies on the bus go
Chatter, chatter, chatter,
Chatter, chatter, chatter,
Chatter, chatter, chatter.
The mummies on the bus go
Chatter, chatter, chatter,
All day long.

*(Open and close your fingers
and thumb)*

The Three Little Pigs

An English folk tale

There once was a mother pig who had three little pigs. They were very poor, and the day came when mother pig could no longer look after the family. She sent the three little pigs out into the big, wide world to seek their fortunes.

The first little pig met a man carrying a big bundle of straw.

"Oh, please may I have that bundle of straw to build myself a house?" asked the first little pig. The man was tired of carrying the bundle of straw so he gladly gave it to the first little pig.

The first little pig built a fine house out of the straw, and he lived there happily. Then along came a big bad wolf.

"Little pig, little pig, let me come in!" shouted the wolf.

"No, no, not by the hair on my chinny chin chin," squeaked the first little pig.

"Then I'll huff and I'll puff, and I'll blow your house down," yelled the wolf. And he did. He huffed and he puffed and he blew the straw house down. The first little pig ran away as fast as his trotters would carry him.

The second little pig met a man carrying a bundle of sticks.

"Oh, please may I have that bundle of sticks to build myself a house?" asked the

second little pig. The man was tired of carrying the bundle of sticks so he gladly gave it to the second little pig.

The second little pig built a fine house out of the sticks, and he lived there happily. Then along came the big bad wolf.

"Little pig, little pig, let me come in!" shouted the wolf.

"No, no, not by the hair on my chinny chin chin," squeaked the second little pig.

"Then I'll huff and I'll puff, and I'll blow your house down," yelled the wolf. And he did. He huffed and he puffed and he blew the house of sticks down. The second little pig ran away as fast as his trotters would carry him.

The third little pig met a man carrying a big load of bricks.

"Oh, please may I have that load of bricks to build myself a house?" asked the third little pig. The man was very tired from carrying the big load of bricks so he gave it to the third little pig.

The third little pig built a fine house out of the bricks, and he lived there happily. Then along came the big bad wolf.

"Little pig, little pig, let me come in!" shouted the wolf.

"No, no, not by the hair on my chinny chin chin," squeaked the third little pig.

"Then I'll huff and I'll puff, and I'll blow your house down," yelled the wolf. And he tried. He huffed and he puffed but he could not blow the brick house down.

"Little pig, little pig, I am coming down your chimney," bellowed the wolf.

"Please yourself," called the third little pig who was busy with some preparations of his own.

"Little pig, little pig, I have my front paws down your chimney," threatened the wolf.

"Please yourself," called the third little pig who was still busy with some preparations of his own.

"Little pig, little pig, I have my bushy tail down your chimney," called the wolf.

"Please yourself," called the third little pig who was now sitting in his rocking chair by the fireside.

"Little pig, little pig, here I come!" With a

great rush and a huge SPLOSH! the big bad wolf fell right into the pot of boiling water that the clever little pig had placed on the fire, right under the chimney. The wolf scrabbled and splashed and scrambled out of the big pot and ran as fast as he could out of the front door. He was never seen again. The third little pig managed to find his two brothers, and they went and fetched their mother. They are all still living happily together in the little brick house.

Jack and Jill

Jack and Jill went up the hill
To fetch a pail of water;
Jack fell down, and broke his crown,
And Jill came tumbling after.

Then up Jack got, and home did trot,
As fast as he could caper.
He went to bed, To mend his head
With vinegar and brown paper.

Pease Pudding

Pease pudding hot,
Pease pudding cold,
Pease pudding in the pot,
Nine days old.

Some like it hot,
Some like it cold,
Some like it in the pot,
Nine days old.

Ducks' Ditty

All along the backwater,
Through the rushes tall,
Ducks are a-dabbling.
Up tails all!

Ducks' tails, drakes' tails,
Yellow feet a-quiver,
Yellow bills all out of sight
Busy in the river!

Slushy green undergrowth
Where the roach swim,
Here we keep our larder,
Cool and full and dim.

Everyone for what he likes!
We like to be
Heads down, tails up,
Dabbling free!

High in the blue above
Swifts whirl and call
We are down a-dabbling
Up tails all!

Kenneth Grahame
1859–1932, b. Scotland

The Gingerbread Man

An English folk tale

One fine sunny day, an old woman was making some ginger biscuits. She had a little dough left over and so she made a gingerbread man. She gave him raisins for eyes and cherries for buttons, and put a smile on his face with a piece of orange peel. Then she popped him in the oven. But as she lifted the tray out of the oven when the biscuits were cooked, the gingerbread man hopped off the tray and ran straight out of the door! The old woman ran after him, and her husband ran after her, but they couldn't catch the gingerbread man. He called out, "Run, run, as fast as you can! You can't catch me, I'm the gingerbread man!"

The old dog in his kennel ran after the old man and the old woman, but he couldn't catch the gingerbread man. The ginger cat, who had been asleep in the sun, ran after the dog, but she couldn't catch the gingerbread man. He called out, "Run, run, as fast as you can! You can't catch me, I'm the gingerbread man!"

The brown cow in the meadow lumbered after the cat, but she couldn't catch the gingerbread man. The black horse in the stable galloped after the cow but he couldn't catch the gingerbread man. He called out, "Run, run, as fast as you can! You can't catch me, I'm the gingerbread man!"

The fat pink pig in the sty trotted after the horse, but she couldn't catch the gingerbread man. The rooster flapped and squawked after the pig but he couldn't catch the gingerbread man. He called out, "Run, run, as fast as you can! You can't catch me, I'm the gingerbread man!"

He ran and ran, and the old woman and the old man, the dog and the cat, the cow and the horse, the pig and the rooster all ran after him. He kept running until he came to the river. For the first time since hopping out of the hot oven, the gingerbread man stopped running.

"Help, help! How can I cross the river?" he cried.

A sly fox suddenly appeared by his side.

"I could carry you across the river," said the fox.

The gingerbread man jumped onto the fox's back, and the fox slid into the water.

"My feet are getting wet," complained the gingerbread man.

"Well, jump onto my head," smiled the
fox, showing a lot of very sharp teeth. And
he kept on swimming.

"My feet are still getting wet,"
complained the gingerbread man again
after a while.

"Well, jump onto my nose," smiled the
fox, showing even more very sharp teeth.

The gingerbread man jumped onto the

fox's nose, and SNAP! The fox gobbled him all up. When the fox climbed out of the river on the other side, all that was left of the naughty gingerbread man was a few crumbs. So the old woman and the old man, the dog and the cat, the cow and the horse, the pig and the rooster all went home and ate the delicious ginger biscuits.

Row, Row, Row your Boat

Row, row, row your boat,
Gently down the stream.
Merrily, merrily, merrily, merrily,
Life is but a dream.

Here is the Church

Here is the church,
and here is the steeple;
Open the door and here are the people.
Here is the parson going upstairs,
And here he is a-saying his prayers.

Link fingers downwards with back of hand facing up to form the church.

Point index fingers up to form the spire.

Turn hands over and wiggle the fingers to be the people.

Doctor Foster

Doctor Foster went to Gloucester
In a shower of rain;
He stepped in a puddle,
Right up to his middle,
And never went there again.

The Lion and the Mouse

A retelling from Aesop's Fables

The lion was very hungry. As he padded through the tall grass, something rustled by his feet. He reached out a great paw, and there was a squeak. He had caught a tiny mouse by the tail.

"Oh please let me go, dear lion," cried the tiny mouse. "I should be no more than a single mouthful for you. And I promise I will be able to help you some day."

The lion roared with laughter. The thought of a tiny mouse being able to help such a huge creature as himself amused him so much that he did let the mouse go.

"He would not have made much of a

meal anyway," smiled the lion.

The mouse scuttled away, calling out to the lion, "I shall not forget my promise!"

Many days and nights later the lion was padding through the tall grass again when he suddenly fell into a deep pit. A net was flung over him, and he lay there helpless, caught by some hunters. He twisted and turned but he could not free himself. The hunters just laughed at his struggles and went off to fetch a cart to carry the great lion back to their village.

As he lay there, the lion heard a tiny voice in his ear.

"I promised you I would be able to help you one day."

It was the tiny mouse! And straight away he began to gnaw through the rope that held the lion fast. He gnawed and chewed, and chewed and gnawed, and eventually he chewed and gnawed right through the rope and the lion was free. With a great bound,

he leapt out of the pit and then reached back, very gently, to lift the mouse out too.

"I shall never forget you, mouse. Thank you for remembering your promise and saving me," purred the great lion.

So the tiny mouse was able to help the great lion. One good turn deserves another, you see?

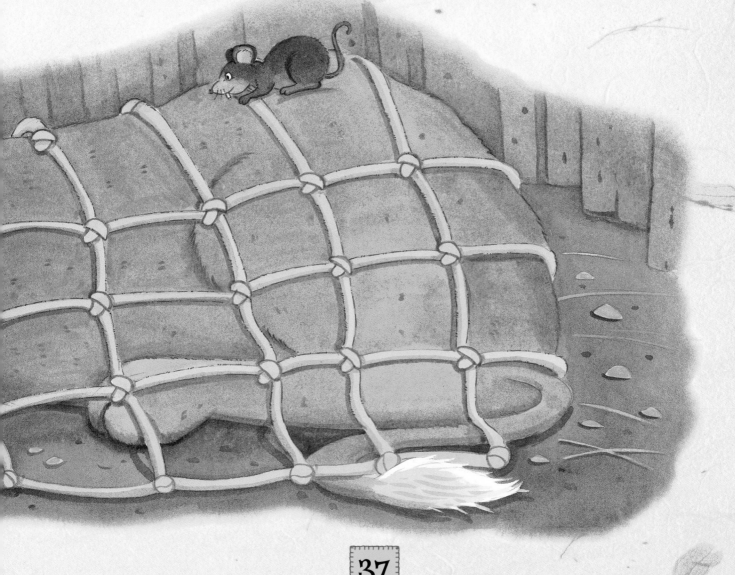

Father's Day

Walk a little slower, Daddy,
Said a little child so small.
I'm following in your footsteps
And I don't want to fall.

Sometimes your steps are very fast,
Sometimes they are hard to see;
So, walk a little slower, Daddy,
For you are leading me.

Someday when I'm all grown up,
You're what I want to be;
Then I will have a little child
Who'll want to follow me.

And I would want to lead just right,
And know that I was true;
So walk a little slower, Daddy,
For I must follow you.

Author unknown

The Twelve Months

Snowy, Flowy, Blowy,

Showery, Flowery, Bowery,

Hoppy, Croppy, Droppy,

Breezy, Sneezy, Freezy.

George Ellis
1753–1815, b. England